This Little Tiger Book Belongs To:

LEON & JAMES RiiSE

from CAROL. CHRISTMAS 2001.

For Mortimer

LITTLE TIGER PRESS
1 The Coda Centre, 189 Munster Road, London SW6 6AW
www.littletigerpress.com
This paperback edition published in 2001
First published in Great Britain 2001
Copyright © 2001 Ruth Galloway
Ruth Galloway has asserted her rights to be identified
as the author and illustrator of this work under the
Copyright, Designs and Patents Act, 1988.
Printed in Italy
All rights reserved • ISBN 1 85430 753 3
1 3 5 7 9 10 8 6 4 2

Fidgety
Fish

Ruth Galloway

Little Tiger Press

London

Tiddler was always fidgeting.

He wriggled and squiggled,

he darted and giggled . . .

until his mum got fed up with him.
"Go out into the sea and swim
till you're tired, but watch out for
the Big Fish," she said.
So Tiddler swam out of his cave.

He dived and he flipped,

he leapt and he dipped.

He sped faster than a rocket . . .

and glided gently like a swan,
letting the sea currents fan his fins.

But he still didn't feel tired!

There were limpets that clung,

and jellyfish that stung.

Tiddler swam on towards
the big, red starfish . . .

and butted it gently with his nose.
The starfish just smiled, so . . .

Tiddler asked the clickety-clackety crab to play, but it scuttled off into the seaweed.

Tiddler came to a big, dark cave.
It looked much more exciting
than his cave back home,
and Tiddler swam in . . .

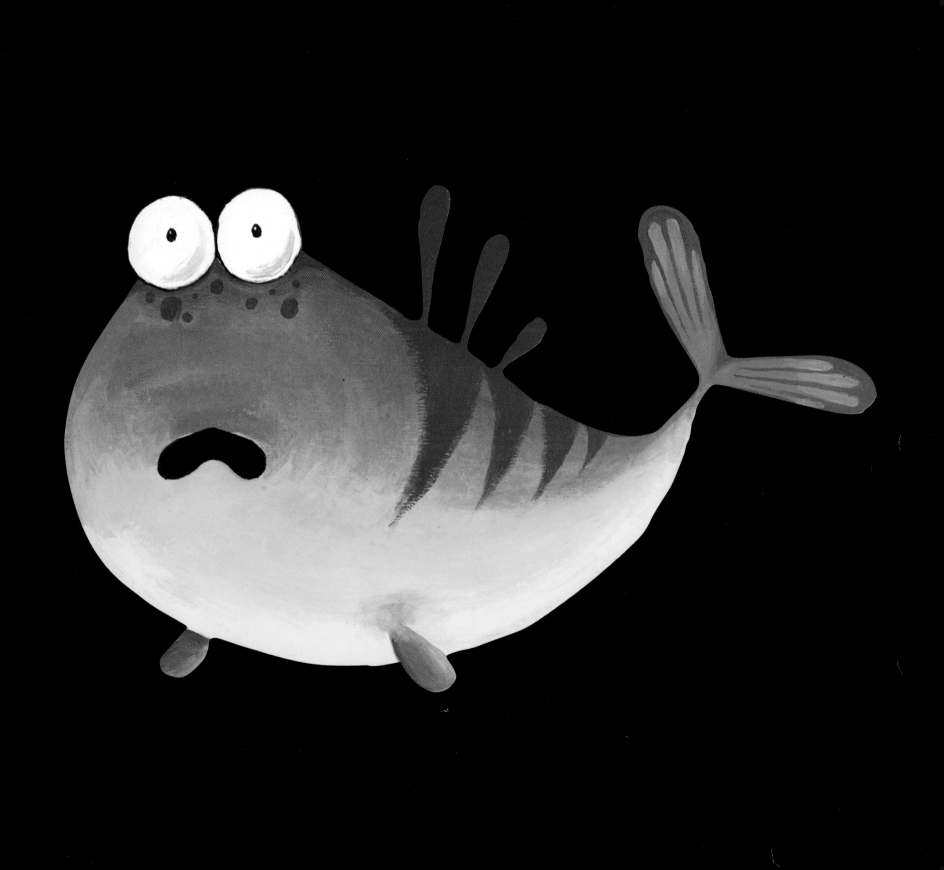

Tiddler was trapped inside the Big Fish!

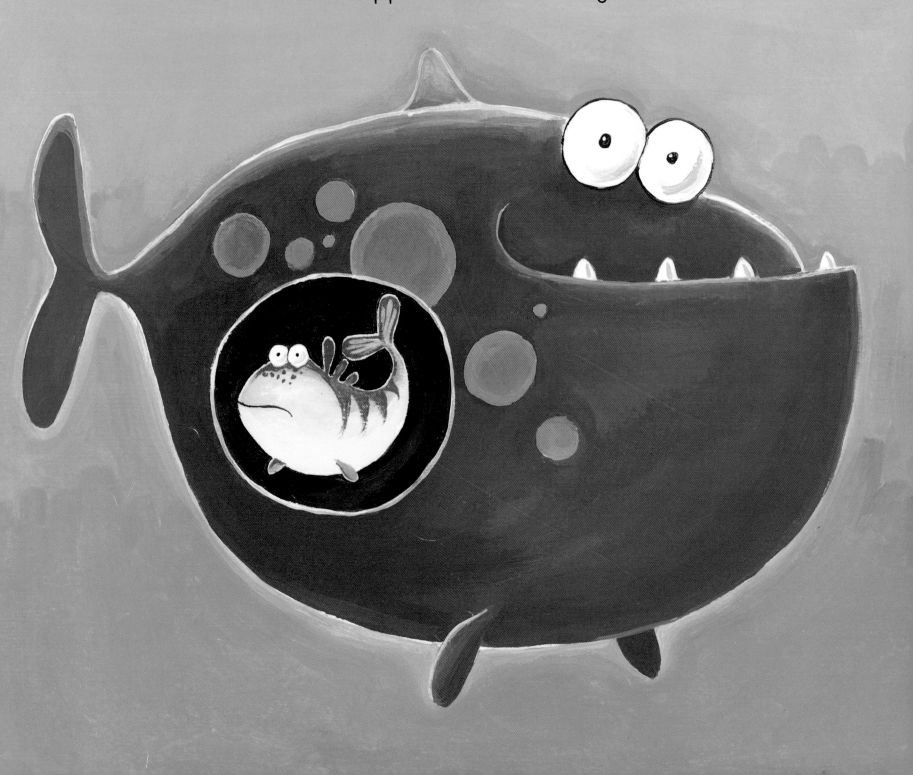

He trembled
and shivered,

and he shook and
he quivered . . .

until the Big Fish's tummy began to feel very
funny indeed.

It rumbled and grumbled,
it turned and it tumbled.
It fluttered and groaned,
and mumbled and moaned.

Suddenly, the Big Fish
did an enormous . . .

out shot Tiddler . . .

past the jellyfish,

and the clickety-clackety
crab hiding in the weeds,

past the starfish . . .

and straight through his own
front door!

"I hope you've used up all that
energy," said his mum . . .

but she would have to wait until the morning to hear about his adventures, because Tiddler was already fast asleep!

Dive into the world of
Little Tiger Press

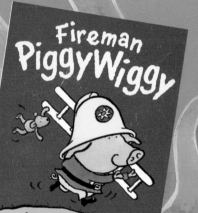

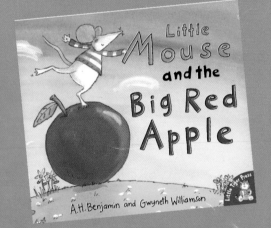

For information regarding any of the above titles or for our catalogue, please
contact us: Little Tiger Press, 1 The Coda Centre, 189 Munster Road, London SW6 6AW, UK
Telephone: 020 7385 6333 Fax: 020 7385 7333 e-mail: info@littletiger.co.uk
www.littletigerpress.com